Abigail

— and 30 —

Wonderful Things

Abigail
— and 30 —
Wonderful Things

Farley Dunn

THREE SKILLET

ABIGAIL AND 30 WONDERFUL THINGS, Dunn, Farley.

1st ed.

 THREE SKILLET

www.ThreeSkilletPublishing.com

Images from:
Public Domain
and/or Hand-drawn by the Author

ISBN: 978-1-943189-81-6

TABLE OF CONTENTS

Preface

Abigail is a very real girl living in a magical house by the sea in the tiny kingdom of Rhode Island. Her grandmother resides in a cozy garden apartment at the foot of the stairs (in a basement that's much more than a basement). Overhead, an apartment hunkers under shadowed eaves, and warm, Portuguese laughter spills from the open windows into the walled garden far below.

Quivering ferns cling to the rock

walls keeping Mr. and Mrs. Mole safe from New England's storms, and a burbling stone fountain whispers secret confidences to the scattered rays of afternoon sun.

Sparrows flit from the pine forest perched on the windswept promontory, and they sing the forest fairies' secrets to the frogs far below.

All-in-all, Abigail leads a pretty perfect life in her Rhode Island house by the sea. She helps her mother in the kitchen, and she counts her father's fingers while he tells her the secrets of tomorrow.

And occasionally, just every now and then, Abigail peers out her windows toward the sea, and when the moon comes out, or the wind blows in a new direction, she sees some very wonderful things.

This is Abigail's story of what she's discovered. When you've finished this tale, I'm sure you'll agree.

Abigail is the luckiest girl in the whole-wide world.

Farley Dunn
South Lee, Massachusetts
May 22, 2019

Abigail and the Glitter Fish

Fish don't float outside the windows of proper Rhode Island houses.

That's what Abigail said when she looked outside her window. Yet, she couldn't deny her eyes, for there it was, looking in at her with its glitter eyes and glitter scales sparkling in the moonlight.

"What are you doing out there,"

Abigail inquired. "This is my house and my air and my yard. You can't be here, you know."

"I know," replied the Glitter Fish, and she took a gulp of Abigail's air, warm and moist from the sea breezes, and opened her mouth to kiss the moon.

"You can't kiss the moon," Abigail reprimanded her. "The moon is mine, too. Every moonbeam that shines in my yard belongs to me."

"It does, does it?" The Glitter Fish adjusted a glitter fin, and with a slight twist of her tail – the tiniest of motions – she turned her back on Abigail.

"You can't do that," Abigail said with a very firm tone in her words. "You must look at me when you speak."

"I'm sorry," the Glitter Fish said, as

she gulped more of Abigail's air, "but it is time for me to go."

"Go? We've barely begun our conversation. You must stay and explain why you are here."

"Count for me, Abigail," the Glitter Fish said, as she drank more of Abigail's air. The moon had begun to dim, and the night was almost gone.

"One, two, three . . ." and by the time she reached ten, only Abigail's house and her air and her yard remained. Oh, and a small amount of moonlight fading into the rising sun.

A Bear Walks on Abigail's Wall

Abigail saw nothing strange about the bear walking on her father's wall. Well, not especially strange, anyway.

See, it was a very strong wall, and it ran right round Abigail's yard. It was of the strongest stone dug from the surrounding soil and encased in sturdy wire frames.

It was a very well-built wall, just right for visiting bears in the middle of the night.

"You there," Abigail called from her open window. "What are you doing on my father's wall?"

The bear sat up and in a very bear-like way (though he took some few moments before speaking) said, "Do you mind if I rest my leg for a bit?" He scratched his knee with very bear-like claws, and dust stirred from his fur.

"Are you a very old bear?" Even Abigail knew this was an impertinent question, but the dust in his fur, well, that could mean old, and it would be good to know.

"Very old," the bear said after he

sniffed the air for a short time, and then he stuck out his tongue to worry the fur at the base of his middle claw.

"As old as my father?" Abigail rested her elbows on the windowsill and paused. The bear could be very slow in answering, but she was prepared to wait.

"As old as your grandmother. Enough questions. You need to sleep. Good night, Abigail."

Abigail yawned, and when she next opened her eyes, the sun was bright through her windows. She thought she found traces of fur on the stone wall, but the breeze grew stiff and blew it all away.

The Night of the Meteor Shower

Unicorns rarely come out to meet with real people. They are used to the tingle of magic in the air, and no one believes any-more, especially in prim Rhode Island.

After all, Abigail didn't believe in

magic, and she had never seen a unicorn, so that must be the way it is.

Then a meteor shower danced across the sky one summer night. The stars fell in shades of blues and pinks, with an occasional green, the sparkling lights tumbling across Abigail's floor and reflecting off her bedroom mirror.

"Ah," Abigail whispered, as she gazed into the night. She had never seen anything so wonderful, not even her birthday cupcakes with sugar sprinkle icing.

"Are you a believer?"

"Who is that?" Abigail leaned out her window to search. "Where are you?"

"On the roof. Can I join you?"

Abigail looked up, and sure enough, just past the edge of the brown-painted gutter, something (or someone!) shimmered with bright light.

"You must," Abigail called. "You certainly can't stay on my roof, not in a meteor shower."

"Meteor shower?" The thing (or person) on the roof laughed. "I prefer magic show. Hold still. I'm coming down."

In a cascade of candy-cane light, a white (and slightly iridescent) unicorn leaped into the air and floated down to Abigail's side.

"Did you come to watch the meteor shower?"

"I am the meteor shower," the unicorn replied with a laugh as she faded into the brightening morning sky.

Two Hummingbirds Have a Tea Party

The flutter of wings woke Abigail from a dream of fairy-tale castles and princes riding white horses.

"Ah, it must be the starlings again," Abigail muttered. "Why do they love my window so much?"

Abigail threw her covers aside and

marched to the window, planting her feet firmly on the polished wooden floor to warn the flighty winged creatures she was on the way to shoo them from the eaves of her house. She flung open her window to a tiny rush of air.

"Why, hello there," a small voice called. "Would you like to join us?"

"Join you?" Abigail searched very hard to see who wished her company. Two tiny hummingbirds hovered just at her windowsill.

"For tea. We're having a party."

"It's the middle of the night." Abigail was still very sleepy, and she blinked twice, the second time very hard. Yes, there on the sill were three tiny cups and a pitcher of steaming tea.

"Is one cup for me?" Abigail hoped,

for she loved tea parties.

"Yes, dear," the second humming-bird (with a red chin and green wings) chirped. "Be very careful. It's my great-grandmother's special teacup."

"Do you have sugar?" Abigail loved her tea very sweet.

"We're hummingbirds, my dear. Always." The tiny birds tittered with laughter as they poured Abigail a cup.

A Bewildered Cat Scratches at the Window

Not everyone knows the secrets of falling and staying on their feet. It's a cat thing, one mastered especially well by a fluffy calico named Delores.

Delores scratched at Abigail's window. She meowed softly, and those who speak cat knew she was saying, "Open up, Abigail. I'm outside, and you're inside."

Abigail lifted the sash – not all the way of course, as Delores had never visited Abigail's window before – just high enough to whisper into the night, "Yes, kitty, what do you need?"

"Meow, meow," which meant, "I'm hungry, and I require a bowl of tasty milk." Of course, anyone who's not silly in the head knows that cats who go by the name of Delores are the cleverest cats in the world, and Delores knew Abigail didn't understand what she meant.

Delores had a plan.

"Meow, meow," Delores said again, which meant, "Watch this," and Delores leapt into the moonbeams caressing the house's back wall.

"Kitty," Abigail exclaimed, and she ran in her stockinged feet right out her bedroom door, down the many steps to her grandmother's apartment, where she slipped outside quick as a flash.

"Meow," Delores said, in a soft and hurt voice, although she wasn't hurt at all. Remember, Delores was especially good at falling and landing on her feet.

"Let me get you some milk," Abigail said, and she poured a bowl from her grandmother's refrigerator and set it just outside the door before slipping upstairs to climb back in bed.

And yes, the next morning, all the milk in the bowl was gone, licked completely clean.

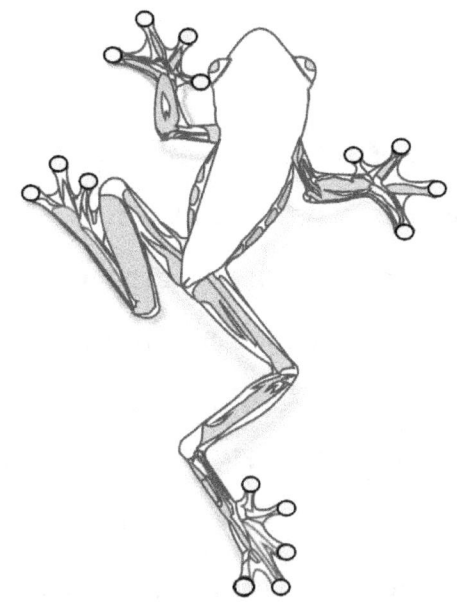

Seafoam and the Tiny Frog

One night the wind blew off the ocean so hard it rattled the glass in Abigail's windows. The trees curled their freshly green leaves and hunkered down, hoping their roots were sunk deeply enough into the ground to hold on until morning.

Ribbons of seafoam fluttered free, released from the ocean waves, floating through the sky, higher, higher, higher.

One especially large piece of foam landed on Abigail's back patio, just where the grass kisses the rock wall her father built. The seafoam shivered for a while, then out crawled a tiny green frog about the size of a shiny new dime.

"Ribbit, ribbit," he called, basking in the sky far overhead. He seemed to be saying, "Abigail, Abigail." In the reflection off Abigail's window, fingers of the spring moon reached down to him, and in their embrace, he imagined the sea.

"Ribbit," he called again, this time

louder, and he hopped with joy to see Abigail's window open just ever so much.

"Ribbit, ribbit," the tiny green frog insisted. "Come to the garden, Abigail. My back is getting very dry."

And sure enough, in a few moments, Abigail appeared at the back door with a small bowl of water, and she set it beside the small green frog.

"There, my little friend. You must have floated on your seafoam boat a long way to find my backyard. I hope you make it home. It's cold outside tonight. I wish you the best," and Abigail pulled her nightgown's collar close and found her way back to her bed.

The Owl in the Tuxedo

"Hoot, hoot." The owl in his fancy-dress clothes strutted along Abigail's windowsill. "Hoot, hoot, Abigail. I've come for your party."

This night, Abigail was far below, having descended a full flight of stairs, walked through her grandmother's apartment, and entered her backyard. Abigail looked up, and she called to the owl, "I've set you a place. It's tea and spice cakes tonight." And sure enough, two plates glimmered on the table, with two cups and a tiny spoon for each.

"Hoot, hoot," the fancy dress called, and he leapt into the air, becoming a dark shape against the moon.

"Don't leave," Abigail called. "Fish. I have slices of fish for you, also."

"Hoot, hoot. I'll be right there." The darkness fluttered with the sound of midnight rose petals and moonbeams, and with no more than a stirring of the air, the fancy-dress owl perched on the back of Abigail's chair. "Hoot, hoot. Where is my fish, my dear? The party is about to begin."

"I'm glad you could come, Mr. Owl.

We will have so much fun." Abigail unwrapped a brown paper package, and out came two slender slices of fresh, pink cod. She laid it on the owl's plate. "From the sea just today, Mr. Owl. See what you think."

"Hoot, hoot. I think I like it very much." Without a further word, the fancy-dress owl snatched the tasty tidbits of cod, swallowed them quick as a flea can jump, and cocked his head as if to say, "More?"

"That's all I brought, Mr. Owl," Abigail said.

"Hoot, hoot," and the owl disappeared without a sound into the night sky.

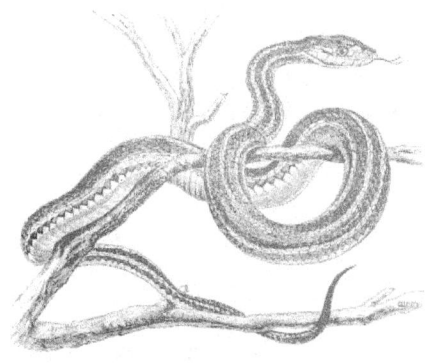

Two Snakes Play a Banjo

A one-handed banjo player is a rarity, indeed. There's a very good reason for it, you see, in that it takes two good hands to play a banjo really well. Of course, anyone can do anything, so there are some one-handed people who do play the banjo very well, but this story isn't about them. This is a story about two snakes who had no hands at all.

Abigail had tried to play her new banjo all day, and she was now very frustrated, as much as when she once tried to ride her bicycle on the ceiling. That is to say, she had no success with her banjo at all.

Abigail admitted she should have been able to play her banjo very well, for she had two good hands (in which she was either very lucky, or she had been very careful), but neither seemed to want to play her banjo even a tiny bit.

Just as Abigail was ready to accept that she wasn't a banjo player at all, in slithered two slender snakes under her bedroom door.

"Can you play the banjo?" Abigail

held it out to them, having asked the question out of frustration (with no expectation that they could). She was surprised when they replied with a nod.

"Of coursssse, sssweet Abigail. Place it on the floor."

Abigail did as asked, and those two snakes entwined themselves around Abigail's banjo. Soon, sweet music poured forth in a tangle of notes too heavenly to be real.

Once their song was finished, the snakes as one said, "You are ssso sssweet, Abigail. Thank you for letting usss play."

They slithered out the door, and that was the last time anyone ever played Abigail's banjo.

A Three-Legged Rat
Gives Abigail a Grin

Everyone drops a morsel of food now and again. Even the most particular person occasionally lets a crumb fall from their napkin, as much as they are embarrassed to admit it.

Abigail sat in her window watching the trees blow in the wind (the reason her windows were firmly and tightly shut), and she snacked on a cinnamon tea cake she had recently begged from her mother.

All cakes have crumbs. It's the nature of a cake, and as we have discussed, Abigail (even though she would never admit it) let one crumb fall to the floor.

This was a very small crumb, if truth be told, but it smelled very good, so good, in fact, a certain three-legged rat decided it was worth crawling out from his hiding place in the wall and directly under Abigail's feet.

"Good afternoon, Mr. Rat," Abigail called. "What do you need today?" (She didn't see the crumb fall, and she had no idea how good it smelled to the rat.)

"May I have a taste of your sweet cinnamon cake, Abigail?" The rat wriggled his whiskers as if to beg for the morsel already on the floor.

"I'm so sorry. I've eaten every bite, and I don't think my mother will give me more." Abigail held up her napkin, and as she said, it was very empty.

"I see a crumb just here," the rat said, his whiskers quivering, and he moved forward on only three feet.

"You most certainly may have anything you find on the floor, but I don't drop crumbs." Abigail pointed her nose high.

"I imagine not, Abigail. I'm sorry to suggest it." The rat grinned as he snatched up the tasty treat and scampered away on his three good legs.

The Chinchilla with a Double Chin

"It's a long way from Chile," Abigail remarked, as if it were normal to talk with a chinchilla.

"I know," said the chinchilla, in his long ears and blue cloak, as if it were equally normal to talk with a girl.

"I don't know that you should be

here. It will be winter someday, and Rhode Island gets very cold." Abigail nodded as if she knew, and she felt she did, for she had lived by the sea her entire life.

"I don't have to live in Chile," the chinchilla said, as he patted his lips carefully with an embroidered tea towel. He folded it and set it aside in a very neat way.

"Where else would you go?" Abigail offered him a tiny sandwich (of mustard and onions on rye), and he took it from her fingers.

"Bolivia. Peru. I have a cousin in Argentina. Perhaps I could live there." The chinchilla nibbled at the sandwich, but it was clear he wasn't really hungry. He was tasting the bread to be polite.

"When will you go?" Abigail frowned at the chinchilla's tenuous nibbles. She had worked hard on the tiny treats. She held up a stern finger in warning.

"After lunch," the chinchilla managed, as he tried to eat the sandwich in two quick bites.

"Good," Abigail said. "I only suggest it because I care. May I pet your tail?"

"Certainly," the chinchilla said.

As Abigail ran her fingers down the chinchilla's long, bushy tail, his two fat chins quivered in excitement at each lingering stroke.

Kerry the Chimp Plays the Bongo

Abigail was studying her French lesson when a raucous noise outside disturbed her very serious train of thought.

"What is that?" Abigail muttered

sternly. "My French lesson is no time for disturbances for which there's no good reason. There had better be a very good reason for all this noise."

She set the thick book aside, and she walked to the window in her argyle feet, muttering things her father would think very bad, indeed, if he overheard. She didn't say them loudly, though, as he was in the next room, and he might be listening. (Fathers always hear those sorts of things. It's something they are trained to do.)

Abigail couldn't be angry when she peered into the garden. There, on the tall, tall stump her father had yet to cut down (another thing fathers tend to do) sat a chimp pounding a set of bongo drums. Abigail lifted the sash with a yank (careful not to break the glass) and called to him, "Who are you, and why are you playing the bongos on my tree?"

The chimp (who went by the name of Kerry, Abigail was to soon learn) paused in his pounding and looked at her. "Kerry, since you asked (I told you she would soon learn his name.), and this tree is my stage. I must play for my supper, and I am very hungry."

"Silly chimp. Stop that commotion and come inside for a banana. I have a French final due."

Kerry got his supper, and more importantly, Abigail received a very good score on everything French that year.

Mr. Komodo Wears a Crown

A king is a very glorious thing to be, with servants, fine food, and castles in which to live. A very grand king has great, long processions through the city streets, where everyone (who's anyone) comes out to cheer and clap their hands.

Mr. Komodo (who was of no real importance at all) had never wanted to be a king, but he occasionally watched the long processions from Abigail's upstairs window, and he wondered about all the fuss.

"Abigail," Mr. Komodo said one day, in his slithery, slippery voice, "would I make a very good king?"

"Of course you would." Abigail had a French lesson due the next day, and she was busy arranging her verb tenses in order of some unimportant importance on a lined sheet of slightly yellow paper. She asked (rather absently, I might mention), "Would you like to be a king?"

"Perhaps," Mr. Komodo whispered, as his long tongue tasted the air, before he slipped it back between his scaly lips. "I think perhaps I would."

"Then we must do that for you."

Abigail stood, her verb tenses still in her hand, and she took her princess crown from the shelf above her bed. "Every king must have a crown. It's the most important thing of all. You may borrow mine."

"It will make me a king?" Mr. Komodo seemed a bit unsure, expecting servants, fine food, a castle, and very importantly, a long procession through the city streets.

"Without doubt." Abigail looked up from her list of neatly conjugated verbs, and with the greatest care, she arranged the crown on Mr. Komodo's head. "Now, you are a very fine king by anyone's measure."

And he was, very fine indeed.

Three Mice Scamper Across the Sill

Windowsills are important for a good many things. Growing a newly planted seed in a paper cup. Displaying a brightly colored piece of sea glass. A book or two, so they are convenient to pick up and read once again. Windowsills are also important for scampering, especially if there is food to be found.

As we know, Abigail occasionally drops a crumb or two from her napkin (though we dare not mention it to her), and from time to time, it lands on her windowsill. It's brought Abigail some very good friends.

"Hello, mouse," Abigail said as she tossed her covers aside and stood. "I see you on my windowsill. Did you have a good night?"

The mouse's whiskers shivered, and he looked expectantly at Abigail, almost as if she had forgotten something. He was very hungry, for he hadn't eaten since Abigail's cookie the evening before. She had dropped a crumb from her napkin, and he had returned home with a very full tummy.

"Have a good day, mouse. I smell

breakfast, and I must be off. I'll see you this evening. Let me give you some light." Abigail opened the window blind, and as she did, three crumbs from last night's cookie fell from her sleeve onto the windowsill.

Abigail didn't see the crumbs fall (and wouldn't have believed it, if she did), but without delay, two other mice joined in the feast, scampering across Abigail's windowsill for their morning meal.

A Scowling Hawk
Frowns at Nothing

Abigail pulled her curtain aside and
searched for the hawk's nest in the big
pine tree on the promontory. The taste of
the sea was in the air, and the wind blew
(as it sometimes does) in great pounding
fists that rattled the shutters on the
windows. She imagined sailing ships on

the sea and great balloons riding high in the sky.

"Screech!" It was Mr. Hawk's way of saying, "Good morning, Abigail," as he launched into flight.

It would be a great day to have wings, Abigail thought, not for the first time that week. She thrust open the window sash, and she waved to the bird landing on her father's tree (which he had yet to cut down).

"Hello, Mr. Hawk. How do you like the wind?"

"Very well," he called back, although his reply was in bird speech, a screech that only birds and Abigail could understand. He lifted his head into the wind, and he held his wings open to catch the air. The tips of his wind-burnt feathers quivered in the stiff breeze.

"How is it to fly today? Can you manage it well?" Abigail had heard the shutters rattle, and she was a perceptive person.

"Very well. Why do you ask?" He hopped two steps between his sentences, as if he needed time to think about his answer.

"The wind is very strong today. That's all."

"Yes, it is." With a frown that told of nothing at all, the hawk beat his wings and launched into the sky, disappearing into the blue expanse overhead.

A Strutting Penguin
Comes to Call

"Is it my birthday today?" The words
tumbled over Abigail's gate and fell
around her like a kaleidoscope of fright-
ened butterflies that doesn't know where

to land, and she looked up in surprise.

"I'm certain it's someone's birthday, but I don't know whose," Abigail called. She had been eating a tea cake and milk, and she pondered her answer very seriously. "Perhaps it's yours. Who am I speaking with, if I may be so forward to ask?"

"Me, oh, it's me, of course. It could be no one else, as no one is with me, besides me, of course."

"If it must be you, then it can certainly be no one else. On that we both agree. Stand back, and I will open the gate."

Abigail lifted the heavy lock (which was never fastened but only appeared to be so) from the locking ring, and she slid the iron bar aside. With a push of her shoulder against the heavy wood, and the creak of rusty hinges (the next thing on her father's list of things to do), the gate swung free.

"Oh, my," Abigail said, stepping back in surprise at her guest. "Do come in. That must be very heavy."

"It is. Only I can know, for I am the only one carrying it. Out of the way, please. Out of the way." In strutted a very small penguin carrying a very large bag of ice and a glass, and it was hard to tell how he could see where he was going. "Point me the right way, please."

"That way," Abigail suggested, tapping him on the shoulder and pointing him straight ahead. There were tea cakes and cookies enough to share.

Abigail Visits with a Tall Giraffe

"There's nothing to do today," Abigail moaned. "My life is very boring."

And so it seemed to the girl who had spoken with a fish, met a very real unicorn, and shared tea with two hummingbirds on her windowsill, for that is the way it works with all of us. The exciting parts are very exciting, and then the real world tries to overshadow our joy with the mundane, everyday things no one can manage to enjoy very much.

"I wish . . . I wish . . ." Abigail began, and then her words faded into silence (but only for a moment, as this was Abigail, who was never very short of things to say). "Is that a . . . giraffe . . . leaning over my fence and eating my mother's pink rhododendrons?"

Abigail rushed down the stairs, gave her grandmother a quick hug (as she always tried to do every time she passed through, unless she forgot), and banged out the back door with no explanation to her grandmother at all.

"Hello."

The greeting rumbled from far overhead, causing Abigail to look up and up and up.

"You are eating my mother's rhododendrons," Abigail said very loudly, wagging her finger in the air to make her point very clear. "You must stop."

"I must, must I?" The very tall giraffe spoke around the pink flowers as he chewed. "They are very good. Besides, that's what rhododendrons are for, eating."

"They are for looking. Now stop!" Abigail said the last word very loudly to make her point.

"I am about finished, anyway. I saw some lovely tulips over on Twenty-fifth Street. I think I'll try those."

Abigail was satisfied, and she headed back upstairs.

The Wind Brings a Hundred Butterflies

The wind is a very unusual thing. You cannot see it, and yet it can travel around the world, hold airplanes in the air, and keep you cool (or warm) at night. Perhaps the *invisibleness* of wind is what misled

Abigail into thinking her life was proceeding as usual that afternoon.

A snowfall had worried the edges of summer just days before, skipping over the warm days of spring, and making it winter all over again. It was too much for Abigail to imagine, and she sat at her window all that lonely day watching the falling snow and wishing it all away.

Then came the butterflies.

The wind had howled all day, doing what it did, rattling the tree limbs and shaking the shutters on Abigail's bedroom windows. It sounded very cold. Abigail sat at her French lessons and tried to ignore it all, remembering the snow from the week before. Surely there wasn't another *storm* on the way to mess up yet *another* day.

"Abigail," her mother called from the kitchen. She was grilling eggplant for dinner, and she peered in Abigail's door. "Look outside, Abigail. See what the wind's brought."

"Not another snow," Abigail wailed. "I cannot bear it again." She put her forehead on her arms to block it all out.

"Don't look then," her mother said. "I have eggplant to prepare," and she disappeared into the kitchen.

Abigail sighed and lifted her head. She turned to the window to find brightly colored butterflies covering the yard and the trees and everything she could see. Then, in a gust of wind that shook the house, they were carried away, and it was just Abigail's yard once again.

A Horse with
Feathered Wings

One day, hoofprints appeared in
Abigail's garden, causing Abigail to ask
herself, "How did a horse's hoofprints get
among my irises?" She didn't know, but it
made her think about how handy wings

would be to a horse. She pondered it constantly over the course of a week, and she decided they would be very handy to any horse that sincerely wanted them. No more leaning over fences because the grass is greener on the other side. No more jumping tall gates to win races for anxious jockeys. No more horseshoes nailed to their hooves.

The very next night, Abigail awoke to a whinny and the pounding of hooves in her yard. She leapt to a window (Abigail was very good at leaping) and leaned outside to the most amazing sight. A horse with a roan coat was standing on its two hind legs nibbling the new growth of a small tree.

"Horse, stop that," Abigail called. She had no patience with animals eating the garden to sticks and stone.

"Neigh," the horse said, which meant, "Oh, you humans."

"How did you get in my garden? The gate is closed," Abigail called, without so much as a blink at her forwardness.

"I am very good at going places no one else can. Goodnight, Abigail." Then he unfurled long, feathered wings and was gone into the night, leaving the garden just as Abigail liked it.

A Fire Phoenix Says
Hello

The firepit in Abigail's garden was a
very fine thing indeed, of metal, rock,
and just the right amount of chimney to
build a good draft. It wasn't unusual to
find Abigail (along with her father of

course) burning up old papers, small sticks, and anything else Abigail thought might catch fire. Even stones, which would sometimes get so hot they cracked when Abigail tossed cold water on the firepit when the night was done.

One night, as Abigail's father stepped inside for a fresh packet of old papers to burn (reminding Abigail to be careful of sparks and asking her to look for a rock for the fire), Abigail discovered a yellow and pink and green stone of very round shape, one she'd never seen before.

"It must be a geode," she whispered to the fireflies in the trees. "It will crack and be beautiful inside, I'm certain."

Abigail tossed the stone in the flames, setting sparks flying (which we won't mention to her father), but rather than crack, the stone caught fire and began to burn. Abigail watched in fascination as the fire danced merrily, and soon, a small bird stood in the ashes from the stone.

"Bird, come out," Abigail said, as urgently as any girl has ever said anything in her life.

"Oh, hello. I can't," the bird said by opening its beak and clattering its tongue against the roof of its mouth. "I'm still growing and getting stronger."

True enough, in moments, the bird was nearly as tall as Abigail. Without warning, the fire phoenix flapped its wings hard, sending sparks everywhere, and it disappeared into the sky.

A Mermaid Swims in the Moonbeams

Moonbeams are especially hard to hold, and they rarely become solid enough to use for a chair. Some very thin people could perhaps sit on them for a short time, but they would have to be very thin and the moonbeam very bright. Moonbeams are much better suited for swimming, especially on bright summer nights when the sky is thick with light, and even walking becomes difficult.

"Abigail, open the blinds."

Shimmering fingers of light tapped at the glass, and the window twinkled with shards of purple, yellow, green, and red.

"I'm busy," Abigail said, and she was, in catching up on her imagination games.

"Open the window, silly girl, and come play." The shimmering fingers tapped again.

"Oh, alright, if I must." Abigail made a pouty face, for she could be pouty at times, but she mostly did as she was asked. Behind the blinds was something she didn't expect. "You're ... a mermaid," she said.

"Of course. Now get that look off your face. The moon won't stick around forever, and we must swim while the light is at its best. Take my hand."

"Your hand?" Abigail was slightly unsure about this.

The mermaid touched Abigail's hand with her fingers of light, and Abigail began to float. The mermaid pulled Abigail through the window.

"What do I do?" Abigail asked. She was floating far above her yard, and nothing was holding her up.

"Swim, like this." The glowing mermaid pushed against a moonbeam and moved forward. "You'll catch on."

And before long, Abigail did.

Abigail Talks with a Red-Crested Dragon

Red-Crested Dragons used to be as common as pennies on a sidewalk (that is, unless you're very poor, and then pennies can be very difficult to find) and Abigail had never seen one. (We're not saying

Abigail was poor, for no one is poor who has such fine parents as Abigail's.) That's why it was a surprise when a Red-Crested Dragon landed in Abigail's garden.

"Hello, Abigail," the dragon said in a voice that spoke of sulfur and brimstone but smelled very much like lemons and custard. Small clouds of reddish smoke puffed from his nostrils with each word. "Have you seen any Red-Crested Dragons today?"

"No," Abigail said. "And why are you smiling? I can tell, you know. Your mouth, it crinkles when you smile. Are you laughing at me? I was having a very nice tea, and that is not very polite."

"Then I shall endeavor not to laugh or even smile at my little joke." The dragon continued to smile despite his promise.

"How do you do, Abigail? I am Rudy, the Red-Crested Dragon. May I take tea with you today?"

"Tea? I'm certain I don't have enough for two." Abigail looked, and she had half a teacake left and only a single cup.

"Look again," the dragon said, burping a red cloud from each nostril, and sure enough, a fresh cake and another cup of tea were on the table.

It was only a matter of time before Abigail's mother called her to lunch, but for a very pleasant few hours, Abigail and the Red-Crested Dragon (who was never seen again, by the way) had a very good conversation about rocks and boys and the smell of the sea on a summer day.

A Turtle Appears in Abigail's Garden

"Oh, what do we have here today?" Abigail (who quite likes turtles and other helpless creatures) shifted a few moss-covered leaves to reveal two black eyes peering at her. "I have never seen you before. Have you come to live in my garden?"

The turtle's mouth moved up and down, and quite understanding what she needed to do, Abigail leaned down very far and put her ear nearly to the turtle's mouth. (See, turtles speak all the time, but people rarely hear them, because a turtle's voice is very quiet indeed.)

"Thank you, Abigail, but I have only come for a visit. I have someplace I need to be."

"Oh, where is that?" Abigail thought her garden was a very nice place to be, and she couldn't see the point of being anyplace else.

The turtle's mouth moved again, and Abigail leaned in very closely. "I wish to visit my brother, and I am on my way to his house. I've been traveling for a full year, and I have a year to go."

Abigail sat up, very surprised. She couldn't imagine traveling a full year to visit someone, much less two. She asked (in her curious way), "Where does your brother live?"

The turtle looked at her and his mouth moved, and Abigail remembered to lean in close. "On Tenth Street."

"But this is Ninth Street," Abigail whispered, keeping her head very low. "You've only a block to go."

"Then I must get started. I don't want to be late. Thank you for visiting with me." The turtle turned and with a great deal of determination and majesty continued his journey to his brother's house.

A Soft-Limbed Spider
Spins a Web

Abigail normally noticed spider webs,
and that's why she was certain there had

been none in the corner of her window just that morning.

"Hello there." Abigail tapped the glass very gently and was pleased to see a brown spider with long, soft limbs appear. "Are you building a web in my window?"

"Obviously," the spider replied, and turned to begin adding onto the web.

"May I ask how long you intend to stay?" Abigail remembered the turtle, and she didn't like her visits to be so brief.

"As long as I like, that is if it's okay with you. Is it?" The spider stopped stringing her web long enough to look at Abigail.

"I suppose so. I may have to raise my window sash from time to time. Will that be a problem?" The summer had grown hot in recent weeks, and Abigail would need fresh air in the house.

"Be careful. I will have babies soon, and they won't know to keep away from your sash. Now, may I get back to work? I must catch some flies, for I have not eaten in some time."

"May I watch you finish your web?" The spider had completed a new section as they talked, and Abigail found the spider fascinating.

"Only if you stop talking. I really must get back to work." The spider scampered across the web to a new section, and in the manner of spiders everywhere, she returned to spinning her web, leaving Abigail to watch her if she wished.

A Wise Toad Makes a Joke

Summer is special in many ways. Fireflies, swimming in the ocean, and cookouts on the beach are a few.

Then there's the summer sounds that

only happen in July, August, and September, those of crickets, baby birds, and toads.

Abigail knew Mr. Toad had come to visit by his calls one night, and in the darkness, she tiptoed down the stairs and through her grandmother's apartment (very quietly so as not to wake her) and through the back door to the fountain. In the distance, the cars of the night workers who had yet to go to bed and the soft whoosh of the ocean at the park said, "Summer's the best time of the year, don't you agree?"

"Mr. Toad?" Abigail called softly, so as not to disturb her grandmother (or her parents, who surely had their windows open). "Where are you, Mr. Toad?"

"Here, my dear, underneath the croak-

uses, the bright yellow ones."

"It's night outside. I can't find you." Abigail knew where the crocuses were, but yellow? She wasn't sure of their location.

"Shall we then play a game of croak-et? The balls and mallets are surely here somewhere."

"Croquet? Not in the dark!"

"Oh? Then a cup of hot croak-co would be nice."

"Mr. Toad, no more jokes." Abigail said very firmly. "Come out for a visit."

"Only if you have Croak-a-Cola."

"I give up. Good night, Mr. Toad," and Abigail went back to bed.

Mr. Platypus offers Abigail an Umbrella

"It's raining outside, Abigail." Mr. Platypus stood on his hind legs (as platypuses often do) and tapped on Abigail's hand with one forefoot. He balanced with his tail flat on the floor, so he wasn't as tall as he could be – but was just tall enough to observe Abigail conjugating her verbs in French.

"I have French lessons to complete." Abigail brushed off his touch and continued to write her words in a very fine and neat order, of which she was certain her teacher would approve.

"But the rain, Abigail. It won't continue forever." Mr. Platypus dropped to the floor and padded to the window seat, where he hopped up and looked longingly out the water-streaked glass.

"That's all fine for you," Abigail murmured absently, as she neatly printed another row of verbs. "You're designed to get wet. I'm a girl, and I'm designed to stay dry."

"Ah, I see the problem." Mr. Platypus dropped to the floor, his forefeet giving a loud splat, and the claws on his hind feet clicking on the wood. He rustled in the closet for a time, calling out a few rude words when things tumbled to the floor, and finally emerged with a long, slender object.

"Abigail, I'm ready to go outside," Mr. Platypus announced with some fervor. "Now, if you please."

"I told you," Abigail started, as she laid down her pencil and turned. She laughed to see Mr. Platypus with an umbrella in his bill.

He nodded and offered it to her, somehow managing to say, "If you please."

The two of them had a very good time in the rain.

The Sad-Eyed Panda's Dance

Abigail wasn't at all surprised to find a sad-eyed panda sitting in her father's fountain with the water running down his white tummy and his eyes closed.

"Hello," Abigail called to him in a cheerful manner. He was her guest, and she would be a bad host to do otherwise.

"Oh, oh!" The panda jerked, his arms

coming up in a defensive posture, as though he felt he could easily be in danger. "Who are you, and what are you doing here?"

"What am I doing here?" Abigail was very surprised at that. This was her house and her fountain, and she had been very cheerful. Now this. She decided she would have to be very firm with her visitor. "I'm Abigail, and you are sitting in my fountain. What are you doing here? Explain yourself."

"Oh, oh, I'm so very sorry." The panda balled his forepaws and twisted them in his eyes. "I'm not crying, really I'm not. I must disgust you, blubbering away in your fountain. I certainly disgust myself. How can you stand to look at me?"

"Now, now, don't be like that, Mr. Panda." Abigail could see the problem easily, as plain as pie cooling on a fence. "You don't disgust me. I like you very much. Besides, disgust can be a very good thing. It protects you from situations where you might get hurt."

"Oh?" The panda sat up and brushed the fountain's water from his face. "It's a good thing when I'm disgusting?"

"You are not disgusting, but it's occasionally good when you feel disgusted. You don't do icky things you'll regret later, like eat an orange covered with mold."

"I would never do that. Thank you. You've made me so happy I could dance." And the sad-eyed panda did just that.

Abigail Finds a Tiger Horse in Her Fence

Abigail walked along the fence around her yard, looking for stories to tell. Sometimes the patterns of the wood told of stars far away, or of the moles living under the promontory. She was surprised to find a section of the fence that was very unfence-like in color, texture, and general grain.

"What is this?" Abigail said aloud. "You are not a fence. You look to be very similar to a horse, if you are similar to anything."

Sure enough, a section of the fence seemed hairier than usual, with an eye, hooves, and perhaps a tail. Could she see an ear sticking up? Abigail thought she could.

"What are you, fence-that-is-not-a-fence, if you're not a horse, which I don't think you are." Abigail admitted to herself this could be a horse, except for the stripes that matched so closely with the pattern of boards in the fence.

The not-very-well-disguised horse-that-was-not-a-horse turned her head to peer at Abigail. "What do I look like to you?" She wriggled her ears, and a shiver ran down her striped back.

"You have stripes like a tiger, but I would call you a horse, except for the stripes, of course. Are you a Tiger Horse?"

"Exactly. Now don't tell anyone I'm here. I'm afraid, and I'm hiding."

"From whom?"

"Shush. Remember, I'm hiding. Go away." The tiger horse shivered all over, and she flicked her ears once.

"You're safe in my yard. No one will bother you here," and Abigail moved on down the fence, gathering more stories to tell.

A Pincushion Porcupine
with an Attitude

"What day is it?" The pincushion porcupine crawled out from under a weeping pine and shook her quills. "Is it the day after Christmas? Has Easter come and gone? Perhaps it's past Memorial Day, and I've missed something important. Oh, my, can someone tell me what day it is?"

Abigail was just setting out the party favors for her birthday (as birthday girls should always do, with no expectations of fancy presents), and she called out, "It's my birthday, of course. Are you here for my party?"

"Party? There's a party today?" The pincushion porcupine rolled into a ball, sending her quills straight out, and she rubbed her hands and feet together. "What else have I forgotten? I didn't bring a present. I don't have an invitation. I shouldn't be here at all."

"Why are you so anxious?" Abigail was never anxious, except once when she was bullied at school, and her father stood up for her (and her mother, of course, though Abigail sometimes had to be reminded). "You are welcome to attend my party, even if you don't have an invitation or bring a present."

"Thank you." The pincushion porcupine unrolled, and she promptly began to cry.

"What now?" Abigail sighed. She had a party to get ready, and this was simply too much.

"People will know I didn't bring a present," the porcupine wailed in self-pity.

"You need to learn to focus your anxiety. That's what my father says. Here. You set the table. It'll do you good."

The porcupine had a fine time for the rest of Abigail's birthday celebration.

A Desert Llama Sings a Song

A stone snicked Abigail's darkened window. As will happen in stories like these, it happened three more times before it got her attention.

"Yes, I'm coming." Abigail stood from her desk (where she was once again conjugating her French verbs underneath a solitary desk lamp) and walked with determined feet to the window. She was just about through with her verbs, and she couldn't waste time on nonsense at her window. She tossed up the sash and called, "I'm here. What do you need?"

"Water," came the long, drawled reply.

"Oh, is that all? I'll be right down." She closed her window (the night had grown cool) and headed down the steps, stopping by the kitchen on the way to fill a bowl with water. Her grandmother was still awake, so Abigail gave her a one-armed hug (the bowl was in the other), being very careful not to spill. Once outside, she called, "Here's your water. I've got lessons to finish. I don't have time to visit."

"It doesn't matter. I'll go away now."

"I don't want that." Abigail's eyes were adjusting to the dark, and she could see her visitor now. "What are you, a small camel or a big llama?"

"A traveling minstrel. I guess you could call me a desert llama. Let me sing you a song." The camel began to grunt, "All alone . . . every day . . . no one around . . . that's all I can say."

"Don't be so depressed. You're a very nice desert llama. I'll get you a second bowl of water."

"Thank you," the camel said, and he began to drink the water in a very noisy and camel-like way until it was gone.

Two Winged Brothers Honk at the Moon

It was the last days of summer (it felt more like fall), and Abigail longingly stood at her window. Flocks of birds were flying south for the winter.

"It's hard to be happy when friends

are saying good-bye," and that's truly the way Abigail felt. She loved summer, and she hated for it to end every time.

In the distance, the sun slowly slipped behind the horizon, and the moon danced into the sky. Two black-and-white birds honked crazily at the rising moon.

"Abigail, Abigail," they called in unison (though it sounded very much like a honk to anyone but Abigail), "the sky is wide, and we have far to go. Come with us."

"I can't, silly birds. I live here. Rhode Island is my home."

"Someday," the winged brothers honked, "you can go anywhere, be any-thing, find your joy in whatever you do. You're only tied here for a time,

Abigail, then every possibility is yours. We'll see you there, Abigail. We'll be waiting. Come join us when you can."

By then, the two winged brothers were disappearing into the darkening sky. The sun was fully gone, and the moon was yellow wax over the ocean. Abigail searched the darkness and remembered the hummingbird tea party, the wide-eyed owl, and the Komodo dragon who wanted to be a king. She thought of the wise toad, the panda, and the tiger horse, and she knew she would do it all, go out into the world and find joy in whatever form it appeared.

Abigail called after the winged brothers, "I'll be there. Someday you'll see me."

And she knew it was true.

Abigail's

story doesn't end here. Check back in about a week or a month or maybe ten years. You'll see all that Abigail's done, because she intends to do it all.